R. S Naylor

Affection's tribute

Original poems

R. S Naylor

Affection's tribute
Original poems

ISBN/EAN: 9783744715195

Printed in Europe, USA, Canada, Australia, Japan

Cover: Foto ©Andreas Hilbeck / pixelio.de

More available books at **www.hansebooks.com**

Affection's Tribute.

ORIGINAL POEMS,

BY

R. S. NAYLOR.

OSKALOOSA, IOWA,
CENTRAL BOOK CONCERN
1874.

PRESS OF

CENTRAL BOOK CONCERN,

Oskaloosa, Iowa.

TO

MY PARENTS

AND

MY FRIENDS

𝕴 dedicate this little bolume

AS A TRIBUTE OF

Affection and Respect.

CONTENTS.

TO OHIO.

I HAVE left thee, dear Ohio,
    But my memory fondly clings
To thy rocks, so high and towering,
    To thy ever-gushing springs;
To thy meadows and thy valleys,
    Where thy crystal waters shine,
To the old hills where the gray rock
    Flashes through the waving pine.

3

In the morning of my childhood
   I have often loved to rove,
When the orb of day was glittering
   From the calm, blue sky above,
To thy forests, where thy songsters
   Sweetly sang their songs of glee.
All these ties, beloved Ohio,
   Bound my youthful heart to thee.

And as I've sat there musing,
   In the shelter of the wood,
On the deeds of those of other days,—
   The great, the wise, the good,—
I, in fancy, stood beside the place
   Where the council fire once shone
On the rude home of the red man,
   In the days that now have flown.

And ofttimes by thy waters,
   When the autumn's gentle breeze

Fanned quietly above my head
    The tall, umbrageous trees,
I've mused, when no sound broke my spell
    But the waves upon thy shore,
And the cadence of those billows
    Only made me love thee more.

And when evening's constellations
    Glittered on thy waters clear,
Warning me that I must leave the place
    So fondly loved, so dear,
I wandered home, when the clamorous
        voice
    Of the day was hushed and still;
No sound broke on my evening thoughts
    But the song of the whippoorwill.

Oh! thou blest land of my childhood!
    Fresh to-day my memory brings

Recollections of thy wild woods,
　　And thy clear and crystal springs;
Still my heart clings to thy forests,
　　With their brown, majestic trees.
Oh! beloved land of my childhood,
　　I do love thee more for these.

Though I love the western prairies,
　　And the ties are stong that bind
My heart to those who have been to me
　　So faithful, true, and kind;
Yet my heart grows tired of noise and strife,
　　And often in my dreams
I go back to the days of my early life,
　　When I sat by thy quiet streams.

LINES PRESENTED TO MY HUSBAND WITH A BIRTHDAY PRESENT.

THE springtime of youth is fast gliding away,
    And the noon of our lives very soon will
        come on.
I look back through the vista of time to the
    days
    That have vanished since our paths in life
        have been one ;

Since the day that we started together to share
    Life's conflicts and conquests, its joys and its
        tears ;
And although we have tasted our portion of care,
    Yet, withal, we must say, they have been
        happy years.

And I praise the kind Giver who dwelleth
 above,
That in His great goodness He ever bestowed
Such a being to cherish, such a warm heart to
 love,
Such a hand to assist me o'er life's rugged road.

And the tears trickle down as I think of the
 time
We no longer shall carry life's burdens together,
When the grim monster Death shall pierce my
 heart or thine,
When the chain that now binds us his sickle
 shall sever.

How lonely the journey will be to the one
 Left alone to contend with earth's sorrow and
 grief;

And naught but the thought that it cannot be
    long
Could afford the sad heart any balm of relief.

Then, dear one, let us live so that when we shall
    part,
  We may feel the assurance of meeting above
In that blissful forever where, heart joined to
    heart,
  We may dwell evermore with the ones that
    we love.

And oh ! let us strive, while together we stay,
  To act toward each other so affectionate and
    kind
That when one from the other is taken away
  No cloud of remorse can o'ershadow the mind.

May the sad, lonely heart be consoled with the
    thought,
  When the form it most loved has been laid
        out of sight,
That the vows made in youth it has never forgot,
  But has done what it could to make life's
        pathway bright.

I THANK THEE, KIND SAVIOUR, FOR TEARS.

WHEN my heart is o'erburdened with sorrow and care,

And my mind overpowered by grief,

And my woe-stricken spirit is seeking to find

The all-healing balm of relief;

When my tempest-tossed bark finds no haven of rest

For its burdensome cargo of fears,

As it sails life's rough ocean, forlorn and distressed,

I thank thee, kind Saviour, for tears.

4

When sober reflection can bring me no joy
  From the grave of the long-buried past,
And the future's dark vista seems paved with
      sharp thorns,
  And by tempest clouds thickly o'ercast;
When the star that once gilded my path o'er
      life's way
  In the heavens no longer appears,
And the light-house of hope seems to die from
      my view,
  I thank thee, kind Saviour, for tears.

When the friends who once met me, when for-
      tune was kind,
  At the altar of friendship to bow,
And brought wreaths of affection my heart to
      entwine,
  Have forgotten to meet me there now;
When misfortune's chill breezes have taken the
      voice

Of affection that greeted my ears,

And the steel words of harshness pierce wounds

    in my breast,

  I thank thee, kind Saviour, for tears.

I thank thee, wise Parent, that thou didst fore-

    know

That afflictions would meet us while here,

Which would sink the weak heart in the ocean

    of woe

If 'twere not for the solace of tears.

And, although for a few fleeting days I am

    placed

In a world full of sorrows and fears,

Thou hast given this means to relieve my sad

    heart ;

  O, I thank thee, I thank thee for tears.

THOUGHTS OF HOME.

I'M lonely, and I feel to-night,
Borne down by melancholy's hand ;
   I wander far from childhood's home,
A stranger in a strange, strange land.

   Oh ! gentle moon, look from thy throne,
And tell, oh ! tell me, dost thou see
   One friend amidst the throng at home
Who thinks and drops a tear for me ?

   Oh ! tell me from thy throne above,
Thou bright and beauteous orb of light,
   Does a father's or a mother's love
Yearn for their child to-night ?

Oh ! does a brother long to see
The playmate of his early years ?

Oh ! does a sister think of me,
And shed in silence bitter tears

For the one who led her infant hand
And joined her in her childish fun ?

Does she think of me in a stranger land ?
Oh ! does she think of the absent one ?

DREAMS OF HOME.

DEAR mother, I've been to the land of
   dreams,
That strange, strange world of mysterious
   gleams,
Where the withered flowers of days gone by
Perfume the dear chambers of imagery.

I saw thee there in that spirit land,
As joyful I stood midst the well known band
Of familiar faces, that brightly shone
With joy as you welcomed your absent home.

You all were there, and your voices clear
Fell like notes of music upon my ear;
And a world of affection pure and deep
Seemed given me in that land of sleep.

Your faces shone with the fire's bright blaze,
As we sat by the hearth of my early days.
A brother's eye sparkled with strange delight,
As he said, I'm so glad you have come to-night.

But the morn has come, and my dream is gone;
I awake with a heart more sad and lone.
Oh! strange, mysterious land of sleep!
Thou hast vanished and left me to pine and
    weep.

O Morpheus, come at the daylight's close;
Bring the eyelids sleep and the mind repose;
But never again bring the land of dreams
To remind me of home and its clear, blue
    streams

For bitter tears from the heart's core come

When I wake to remembrance, at morning's
      dawn,

And find it's a dream that has vanished by

And left my visions of home to die.

LINES WRITTEN ON THE BLANK LEAF OF A BIBLE PRESENTED TO MY LITTLE DAUGHTER ONE YEAR OLD.

MY darling May, bestowed by Heaven
  To light life's dark, bewildered road ;
Thou gem of love, so kindly given
  To lead my wandering soul to God ;
    To thee I dedicate this gift
    That points the only glorious way
    That leads to life and perfect peace,
    And everlasting day.

I give it with a heartfelt prayer,—
   A mother's prayer, devout, sincere,—
That thou mayest learn the many truths
   That God has wisely planted here.
      My infant, thou dost little know
      The joy, the fear, the hope, the dread
      That thrills thy mother when she feels
      That thou hast youth's wild paths to tread.

To tread, if God shouldst will that thou
   Shouldst come upon the busy stage
Of human life to act the part
   Of youth, of girlhood, and of age.
      How that may be I cannot know;
      Perhaps e're morning's light shall come
      Thy soul may soar to spirit worlds.
      God's will be done—forever done.

But should He spare thee yet to read
  The volume which thy mother gave,
When the frail form that first thou knew
  Lies moldering in the silent grave,
      I charge thee by the silken cord
      Of love that binds my soul to thee
      To give thy heart unto the Lord,
      And live but for eternity.

EVENING THOUGHTS.

O HOW pleasant to me is the still hour of
    evening,
  When the shadows of twilight come stealingly
    on,
And the soft, gentle breeze fans the warm brow
    of heaven,
  When the great king of daylight has vanished
    and gone;
When nature's loud voices are hushed into quiet,
  And the husbandman's labor is brought to a
    close ;
When this great active world's busy tumult and
    riot
  Into stillness is hushed by the hand of repose.

As I sit by my fireside, the lamp brightly burn-
ing,
My thoughts wander back o'er the work of
to-day
That has passed to that bourne whence no trav-
eler's returning
Has ever illumined our wandering way.
Oh! thou day just departed on time's fleeting
pinions!
What news hast thou borne to that fathomless
sea
Of my sins of omission, my deeds of transgres-
sion?
Oh! what is the message thou bearest of me?

Hast thou borne on thy pinions the wailing of
sadness?
The groans of the suffering my hand might
have stilled?

Or were thy wings laden with sweet songs of
    gladness
  From mouths of the hungry I caused to be
    filled ?
Oh ! thou great book of fate, thou record of
    ages!
  What hast thou to tell of my actions to-day ?
What black marks of sin are inscribed on thy
    pages
  To be read in the finis with fear and dismay ?

When my fancy peruses that great book of
    actions
  From the story there written I fain would
    depart ;
For methinks that that dreaded herculean
    volume
  Is filled with the numberless sins of my heart.

And so seldom are scattered my few deeds of
    goodness;

Along through the story of my useless past,

That my heart seems to shrink from that sure,
    truthful record,

And by sad, dark forebodings my soul is o'er-
    cast.

O, thou great king of day! when again thou
    hast risen

To waken a slumbering world out of sleep,

May I start in the straight, narrow pathway of
    duty

And all God's commandments so faithfully
    keep

That when darkness again shall preside o'er the
    billow,

Or night's radiant queen take her watch o'er
    the sea,

May I sweetly repose on my soft, thornless
    pillow,
And feel that this world is the better for me.

DEAR brother, though the critic's lip
    May proudly curl and sneer
At the unstudied, uncouth rhyme
    That I have written here,

I hope for better things from you
    Who know my heart's intent ;
Who know these lines were only penned
    For youth's encouragement.

I am your senior, and should by
    Experience be more wise.
Then do not deem it rash in me
    To drop you this advice.

You'll find youth's path a slippery one,
    And, if you're not aware,
You'll slip from virtue's narrow track
    Into temptation's snare.

Sometimes you'll find in it a rose,
    And oftentimes a thorn
That goads the tender heart with shame,
    And leaves it sadly torn.

If you will only pluck the flowers
    Of knowledge, love, and truth,
In after years you may look back
    Upon a well spent youth.

But if you leave the path of right
    To pluck the thorns and flowers
Of idle pleasure, you'll look back
    With pain on childhood's hours.

You'll find its roses soon will fade
　And leave you naught but thorns
To cull in winter's gloomy age
　And probe the heart that mourns.

You'll meet with those who seek to lure
　You from truth's path of light ;
But show them works to prove that you
　Are standing for the right.

Mingle not with such : you little know
　The influence it may have ;
For those who see you oft with rogues
　Will mark *you* for a knave.

No ; rather seek for friendship
　With the forest, vale, or brook ;
Or at the shrine of solitude,
　With some kind, teaching book,

Search deep for wisdom's shining ore
   That foes can ne'er destroy,
And keep it bright with earnest toil,
   And free from all alloy.

And, as you sail down Time's swift stream,
   Strive hard to keep your bark
In duty's path, and leave behind
A bright and shining mark;

A mark to shine and ever gild
   The path you trod on earth;
A name to live and ne'er disgrace
   The land that gave you birth.

SLANDER.

O MAN! let reason's power tame
  That venomous tongue, that fiery lust
That publisheth thy neighbor's shame,
  But leaves his good deeds in the dust.

Oh! let his deeds of virtue fly
  On immortal wings, and ever live;
But leave his deeds of shame to die
  And molder in oblivion's grave.

NIGHT THOUGHTS.

'TWAS evening. On the rocky hill
  The moon looked down in tender love ;
The ocean wave was hushed and still ;
  The sky was blue and calm above.

The stars put forth their gentle light
  To cheer their radiant, beauteous queen.
I gazed with rapture and delight
  Upon the charming, lovely scene.

Oh! was it wrong that I should pine
   For eagle's wings to soar away
Where lights like these forever shine
   With steady and undimming ray?

Who would not leave a world of woe,
   Where beauty flees with fleeting time,
And to those charming regions go
   And like those stars forever shine?

Yet pause, my soul, art thou aware
   That mortals stained by guilt and sin
May strive to make an entrance there,
   But cannot, cannot enter in?

Art thou not marked by many a crime
   That bath not been forgiven?
And wouldst thou enter that fair clime
   And mar the peace of Heaven?

Ah, no ; I'd rather stay below,
  With creatures weak and frail like me,
Than carry guilt and sin and woe
  Where they should never be.

But when my robes have been washed white,
  And all my crimes forgiven,
Then I would join the saints in light
  And shine on earth from Heaven.

TO A SNOW BIRD.

O COME to my window,
  Thou beautiful bird!
Thy sweet little note
  Is the only I've heard
Since the summer and autumn
  Have vanished and gone.
All the others have left thee
  To warble alone.

O come to my window !
    The tempest's wild storm
Will certainly shiver
    Thy beautiful form.
I'll give thee protection
    From snow, sleet, and rain,
And when thou desirest
    I'll free thee again.

Dost thou ask, little bird,
    Why I love thee the best,
And why thou art dearer
    To me than the rest ?
When the others have vanished
    With sweet summer's bloom
Thou cometh to cheer me
    In winter's sad gloom.

I've had friends, little bird,
  That would stay very near
To my side until tempests
  And storms would appear;
But when fortune's bright sunshine
  Had settled in gloom
Those friends quickly left me
  Alone to my doom.

I too have had friends
  Who were faithful and true,
Who would stay through life's sunshine
  And misfortunes too;
Who closely would cling
  When life's sunshine was warm,
But closest would cling
  · In its tempest and storm.

DARE TO DO RIGHT.

FELLOW-MORTALS, as you journey
   Down the ebbing stream of time
To the sacred bar of judgment,
   There to answer for each crime,
Let the voice within direct you
   Through life's scenes of dark and light ;
Listen to its solemn teachings,—
   Do what conscience says is right.

It will teach you, if you'll listen
   To its still and quiet voice,
What's the path of right and duty,
   Though it may not be your choice.
And in cases where temptation
   Lures you from truth's path of light,
Lay aside your will and wishes,—
   Do what conscience says is right.

TO MY OLD PLAYMATE.

I'VE been sitting by my window
  In the moon's soft, gentle light,
Thinking of the past and friends beloved
  Who are far from me to-night.

I've been wondering if thy memory
  Is as faithful unto thee
In bringing gone-by scenes to view
  As mine has been to me.

Mine has brought the ancient meadow,
    Where we often used to go
In winter with our little sleds
    To slide upon the snow.

It has brought the little playhouse
    That we built upon the rock,
With its carpets and its beds of moss,
    And its roof, the hoary oak.

There we spent the hours of summer,
    When we were young and fair ;
But for our future years we built
    Bright castles in the air.

On the rock upon the hillside
    Our playhouse still doth stand,
But the castles that we built for age
    Were only built on sand,

And the waves of time came swiftly,
   And from off the sandy shore
They washed youth's bright airy castles
   From our view forever more.

We have learned that life is real
   And of sterner stuff is made
Than our youthful visions pictured
   From the future's brilliant shade.

Thou hast given to another friend
   Thy hand, thy love, thy life ;
Thou hast tried life's stern realities,—
   Thou hast become **a** wife.

And I would not have thee falter
   In thy love for that true one
Who has linked his fate for life's short day
   With that which is thine own.

I have bowed at that same altar,
   And have vowed to ever love
One dearer than all other friends
   Except the Friend above.

And may that Friend in Heaven
   Send misery, want, and shame,
If I prove inconstant to my vow
   Or e'er disgrace his name.

But why should ties be severed
   That were formed in childhood's breast,
Though thy home is in an eastern land,
   Mine in the prairied west.

Let the silver cord that bound us
   In those happy days of yore
Grow stronger with the growing years,
   And bind us evermore.

Yes, evermore remember me
  As thy firm and faithful friend,
And while apart let our tongues be
  The ever-faithful pen.

THE STREAM OF TIME.

WE are gliding down the stream of Time,
　　Like ships upon the sea ;
We're striving for that blissful clime
　　In the blest eternity.

We're sometimes tossed by adverse seas
　　Which drive us from the way
That leads to life and perfect peace
　　And everlasting day.

But if our captain is the Lord
　　We need not fear its power ;
He calms it at a single word
　　And quells its awful roar.

Then let us choose Him for our guide
　　Down the rough stream of Time,
That our frail barks may smoothly glide
　　To Heaven's celestial clime.

BEAUTY OF THE MORNING.

WHEN the shades of night are flying
  From the dazzling orb of day,
And the lark its wing is hieing
  Upward on its heavenly way,

Then I rise with joy and gladness
  From my couch of sweet repose,
And I banish grief and sadness
  With life's many cares and woes.

I look around with admiration
  On the meadow, hill, and wood,
And see the beauties of creation
  Made by Him so wise and good;

And then I think how thankful ever

I should strive to live and be

To the great and bounteous Giver

Who has been so kind to me.

EVENING.

THE harvest moon is shining bright
  O'er nature's sweet repose ;
No cloud obscures the mellow light
  That gilds the summer rose.

But hushed and still all nature seems ;
  Each passion sinks to rest
From daylight's toils and various schemes
  That agitate the breast.

THE SOUL.

THE mountain tall must waste away,
  The forest oak must bend;
The flower is subject to decay
  Who marks it for its friend.

The man of high ancestral birth,
  The man of pride and lust,
Must yield his body to the earth :
  Dust must return to dust.

But the soul, Immortal, in its prime
  Shall never, never die,
But live throughout the boundless time
  Of all eternity.

DEDICATED TO MY FRIEND ON THE

DEATH OF HER CHILD.

SHE hath passed away from all earthly sad-
   ness,
 From sin and suffering, from pain and woe,
To that blissful region where joy and gladness
 Like mighty rivers forever flow.
Her spirit has gone where the soul's elysian
 Never crumbles with sickness or sad decay ;
From terrestrial woes to the joys of Heaven
 Her tender spirit hath passed away.

She has passed away, and your hearts are lonely ;
   You'll miss her voice in the quiet eve ;
The morn will come, but its coming only
   Brings dreary memories to make you grieve.
The noonday sun, with its beauteous beaming
   Will gild our earth with a radiance bright,
But your hearts are sad, and its splendor gleam-
        ing
   Cannot enter in with its cheerful light.

She has passed away, and the dews of autumn
   To-night are falling around her bed ;
She has heard the voice of her Saviour calling,
   She has joined with the blessed, the early
       dead.
Grieve not for the loved so early taken
   By the frosts of death to her final home ;
For years will pass like a fleeting phantom,
   And you may join in the world to come.
9

She hath passed away with the mild September,

    Like a tender flower beginning to bloom.

But breath not a sigh : lone mother, remember

    Her spirit hath passed beyond the tomb

To that happy land, to that blessed Saviour

    Who called his lamb to the other shore ;

And when you lament your absent daughter,

    Remember the skies have one angel more.

TO THE FLOWERS.

LOVELY flowers of sunny summer,
  Can it be that ye have gone
Like a transient, fleeting shadow,
  From the hillside and the lawn?

Can it be that ye have vanished
  Like a vision of the mind,'
Like a passing gale of autumn,
  Like a cloud before the wind?

In vain I seek you in the valleys,
  In vain I search the leafless grove,
In vain I wander o'er the prairies;
  I cannot find the flowers I love.

Ye missing treasures of the summer
   That bloomed to beautify the earth,
Why have you left the breeze that loved you,
   The dust that gave your soft germs birth?

In vain I call you, gentle flowers;
   Ye fear old tyrant winter's reign;
But when he leaves the lawn and hillside
   Will you not lift your heads again?

Adieu, fair flowers! The hope that lingers
   To cheer my heart since you have fled
Proclaims in loud and thrilling accents
   That spring will resurrect the dead.

HOPE.

HOPE silently stole to the bed of disease,

And the sufferer's frown changed to calmness
and peace.

She went to the dwelling of sorrow and sadness,

And soon from that dwelling came sweet songs
of gladness.

She led the young tyro up the steep path of
fame,

And would not desert him in sickness or pain,

But stayed by his couch till life's last link was
riven,

And when he left earth she went with him to
Heaven.

THE CHURCHYARD.

PAUSE by yon churchyard, thoughtless
youth !
  Pass not thus careless by.
Here is the place, says solemn truth,
  Where all must shortly lie.

Pause and reflect, gray, sober age !
  The tide of time ebbs fast ;
'Twill wash thee from life's busy stage,
  And launch thee here at last.

TO THE EVENING STAR.

PALE evening star, with gentle spark,
  O come and bid our labors fly ;
Guide home the wanderer through the dark
  When evening closes daylight's eye.

Conduct my thoughts, sweet star, above
  The many cares of human life,
Where angels light each face with love,
  And ever banish mortal strife.

And while we're journeying to the tomb
  In this thick wilderness of tears,
Amidst the world's perplexing gloom,
  O light our darkened clouds and fears.

Guide us, sweet star, while here we stay,

In paths of righteousness and love ;

And when our spirits leave their clay,

Pale evening star, light them above.

THOUGHTS BY THE OCEAN.

THERE'S beauty in thy curling stream
That charms like fancy's morning dream ;
It lulls the senses, charms the ear,
And stills the nerve from torturing fear.

There's sadness in thy solemn tone
That echoes to the widow's moan
Of sorrow for the lost and brave
Who have found in thee a watery grave.

There's terror in thy threatening wave
That quells the heart, though stout and brave;
When tempests beat against thy breast
Thou art in awful terror dressed.

There's music in thy murmuring roar

When storms have left thy shelly shore;

It comes from where thy sea nymphs dwell,

Like music from some coral shell.

I WATCH FOR THEE.

'TIS evening, and the shades of night
   Are stealing o'er the lea ;
The fire upon the hearth glows bright:
   I wait and watch for thee.

The sun's last ray shines dimly on
   The distant forest tree,
The canary now has hushed his song:
   I list and watch for thee.

I hear thy footsteps on the street,
   My heart throbs joyfully ;
I watch no more but bound to meet
   The smile thou hast for me.

I knew when daylight's task was done,

And thou from labor free,

That thou wouldst quickly hasten home

To her who watched for thee.

A WAKE, my soul, to labor, for the day is
    dawning;
The silent wheels of time are rolling fast,
And soon will bring the shadows of the evening,
    When the time to labor will be over past.

And shall the evening find my task neglected,
    The deeds of love I might have done un-
        wrought,
And naught but idleness to my mind reflected,
    For deep investigation, bitter thought?

Ah, no; I would not live a life so aimless
  That none would ever miss me when I'm
    gone,
I would not leave this busy stage of action
  With life's great purposes undone.

But I so faithfully would do my every duty,
  Performing all the work to me assigned,
That all would say, when my life work was
    finished,
  She did the best she could to bless mankind.

And when I cross death's cold and chilling river,
  O may I rest, when life's hard race is run,
At home in Heaven, where I can hear my
    Saviour
  Saying, my child, well done, well done.

TO MY INFANT SON.

AS I hold thy chubby hand in mine
  And gaze upon thy face,
So innocent, so pure, where time
  Hath left no furrowed trace,
I press thee fondly to my heart
  And breathe the earnest prayer
That sin, with its vile, poisonous dart,
  May leave no traces there.

Thou canst not know, my little one,—
    Joy of my heart and life,—
My feelings when I think thou soon
    Must join earth's scenes of strife
And battle with its many cares,
    Its thousand foes to meet,
And be exposed to all the snares
    That are laid for little feet.

When I see thy face beam with that smile
    I scarce can think that thou
Can e'er be led in paths of guile,
    Or be less pure than now.
And yet I know thou art not divine,
    Thou art mortal, prone to stray,
And, like the rest of human kind,
    To miss truth's narrow way.

But O may He whose mighty power
   Contracts the raging seas
Lead thee, dear boy, forever more
   In paths of right and peace.
O Saviour, guide those little feet
   In the way thyself hath trod
Until they walk the golden street
   In the Paradise of God.

WE WHICH HAVE BELIEVED DO ENTER INTO REST.

WE talk of our rest in the sky,
  Of the joys of that region so fair,
And ofttimes grow weary and sigh
  For the rest that awaiteth us there.

We speak of the river of life,
  That makes glad the whole city of God,
We rejoice that the world's busy strife
  Never enters that quiet abode.

But how often, I fear, we o'erlook
  The sweet Heaven we may have in our
      breast,
For the Saviour has said in his book,
  That they who believe do have rest.

That the strong iron shackles of sin
   No longer shall fetter the soul,
That those unholy passions within
   No longer the heart shall control.

For the Saviour has made it his home,
   He bids its wild conflicts all cease ;
Its affections no longer shall roam,
   But, centered on him, shall have peace.

I would not have us love Heaven less,
   But I would that the whole world might
      know
That God's kingdom may be in our breast,
   And that Heaven may begin here below.

For I ever shall praise our dear Lord,
   As long as life throbs in my breast,
That he ever has said in his word
   That they who believe *do have rest.*

INVOCATION.

COME, muse, 'tis midnight's quiet hour ;
   The mists of night are thick and deep,
And Morpheus, with her awful power,
   Has wrapt a drowsy world in sleep.

O bring me visions bright and fair,—
   Visions of peace, of joy, and rest,—
To drive away the anxious care
   That agitates my throbbing breast.

Come, muse, and to this troubled heart
  That sinks beneath its weight of woes
Bring thoughts that bid all gloom depart,
  And hushes into sweet repose.

Dispel the clouds that overcast
  My tired mind, and bring, oh ! bring
Some bright remembrance of the past
  To lift my spirit's drooping wing.

Oh ! help me, in the time to come,
  Bravely to meet earth's pain and strife,
To look midst scenes of deepest gloom
  Upon the sunny side of life.

TO THE LOVED AT HOME.

FATHER, mother, sister, brother,
  Far from you to-night I roam
In a distant land of strangers,
  Far from childhood's early home.

Far from scenes beloved in childhood,
  Far from kindred ties of love,
Far from sunny haunts of pleasure,
  Where in youth I loved to rove.

Autumn winds to-night are blowing,
  (From Pacific's shore they come),
Wafting breezes of affection
  To the ones I loved at home.

O may heaven's gentlest breezes
   Waft you peace upon their wings,
And affection's bright dew moisten
   Flowery scenes where memory clings.

Flowery scenes which faithful memory
   Brings me from my native land,
And she helps me cull the treasures
   With her slender, magic hand.

Hasten, breezes! bear the message
   That my heart sends forth to-night
To the fondly cherished loved ones,
   When dull Morpheus takes her flight.

Tell them, though I oft have wandered
   In forbidden paths and wild,
God has ever dealt in mercy
   With their absent, erring child.

LINES WRITTEN UNDER MY PICTURE.

MY soul, let not earth's scenes entwine
  Around thee with their transient joys ;
Its glittering treasures all combine
  To draw thee from thy native skies.

But O, my soul, forever pray
  That all the powers God has given
May be engrossed each passing day
  In laying treasures up in Heaven.

THE END.